W9-DES-304
3 0036 01399 3256

THE NIGHTMARE BRIGADE

PAPERCUTZ

MORE GREAT GRAPHIC NOVEL SERIES AVAILABLE FROM

PAPERCUTZ™

THE SMURFS TALES

BRINA THE CAT

CAT & CAT

THE SISTERS

ATTACK OF THE STUFF

LOLA'S SUPER CLUB

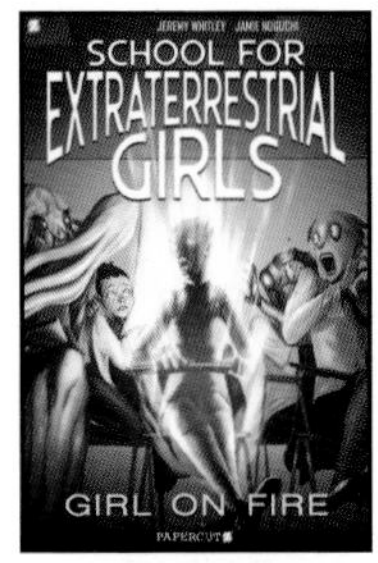

SCHOOL FOR EXTRATERRESTRIAL GIRLS

GERONIMO STILTON REPORTER

THE MYTHICS

GUMBY

MELOWY

BLUEBEARD

GILLBERT

ASTERIX

FUZZY BASEBALL

THE CASAGRANDES

THE LOUD HOUSE

ASTRO MOUSE AND LIGHT BULB

GEEKY F@B 5

THE ONLY LIVING GIRL

papercutz.com

Also available where ebooks are sold.

THE NIGHTMARE BRIGADE

The Girl from Déjà vu

Story
FRANCK THILLIEZ

Art
YOMGUI DUMONT

Color
DRAC

PAPERCUTZ
NEW YORK

THE NIGHTMARE BRIGADE

#1 The Girl from Déjà vu

Story: Franck Thilliez
Art: Yomgui Dumont
Color: Drac
Color Assistance: Reiko Takaku
Dossier pages: Géraldine Martin

JayJay Jackson — Production
Joe Johnson — Translation
Wilson Ramos Jr. — Lettering
Spenser Nellis — Marketing Coordinator
Jeff Whitman — Managing Editor
Jim Salicrup
Editor-in-Chief

Special thanks to Clélia Ghnassia & Moïse Kissous

HC ISBN: 978-1-5458-0876-4
PB ISBN: 978-1-5458-0877-1

Printed in China
February 2022

Papercutz books may be purchased for business or promotional use. For information on bulk purchases please contact Macmillan Corporate and Premium Sales Department at (800) 221-7945 x5442.

Distributed by Macmillan
First Papercutz Printing

JULES FERRY HIGH SCHOOL

Oops! Sorry...
POF

Wimp on wheels.

What a pair of morons!
Forget about it, ESTEBAN.

Oh, there's my dad.

PROFESSOR ALBERT ANGUS found me in this immense forest three years ago.

Sleep Clinic
I don't remember my past anymore.

ANGUS CLINIC
Or who I am really, or where I'm from...

Albert raised me as his son, and TRISTAN welcomed me like a brother.

They're my only family.

Together, we help young people like ourselves to recover from their terrible dreams.
We're the "NIGHTMARE BRIGADE."

We have work tonight.

SARAH, 14 years old, parents getting divorced...

For weeks, she's been suffering from a nightmare that's been plaguing her almost every night.
What kind of nightmare?

We don't really know. She only has vague memories of it.
A city, snow, empty, abandoned streets...
Then she wakes up in a sweat, screaming.

Her mother tried everything before coming here.

Well, she should've come here first!

In the meantime, read this closely and go get yourselves ready.
We'll meet in two hours.
POF

And that sheet there?

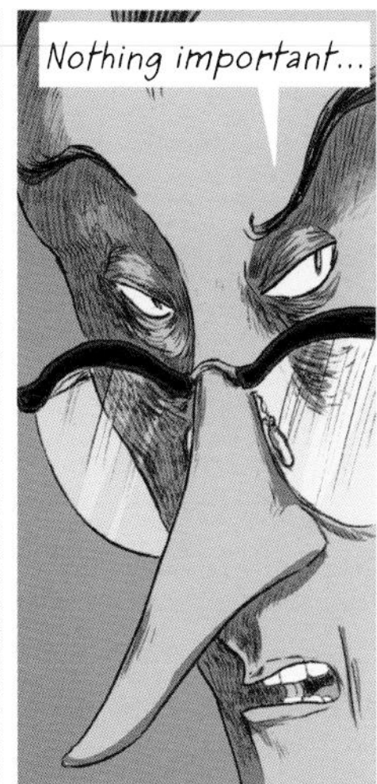
Nothing important...

Don't be late!

SLAM

That's weird.

I feel like I've seen this Sarah before...
Maybe from before your memory loss?

Maybe, yes... Maybe...

Good evening, Professor.
Good evening.

As you can read, Sarah has been an amnesiac for three years, exactly like Esteban.
102
SLEEP ZONE SILENCE!

Her adoptive parents found her wandering in the forest.
STAFF ONLY

I feel like I recognize her.

That's not just a feeling. That's her. Without a doubt.
Does Esteban know?

No, ELISA... It's better he doesn't know.

Good evening, Sarah.

I'm Professor Angus.

I heard you can get rid of nightmares.
How do you do that?

These sensors connected to your skull will allow us to analyze your brain waves...

And these big spool things everywhere will help send messages to your brain while you sleep.
It's kinda scary.

Not at all. All you have to do is relax and let yourself fall asleep.

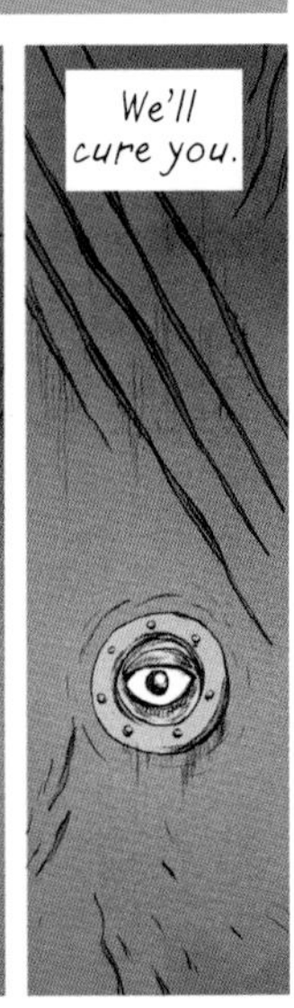
We'll cure you.

DZZZ
We're here in the airlock.

We enter kids' nightmares through here...
1) TIME PASSES 24X FASTER IN THE NIGHTMARE.
1 HOUR IN REALITY
→ 24 HOURS IN THE DREAM
2) NEVER FORGET TO CLOSE THE DOOR BEHIND YOU!
3) EVERYTHING BECOMES TRULY REAL FOR YOU ONCE YOU'RE ON THE OTHER SIDE.
DZZZ

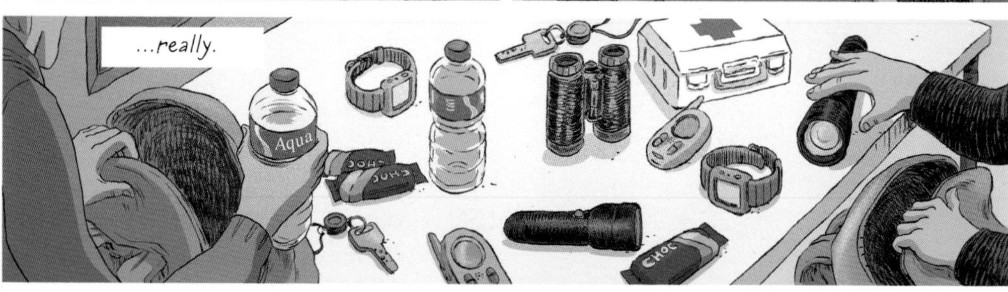
...really.
Aqua
CHOC
CHOC
CHOC

It seems the professor has already tried to send experienced adults like ELISA into patients' minds...

...But it didn't work out right.

The children's brains detect their presence.
Blip Blip
Blip Blip

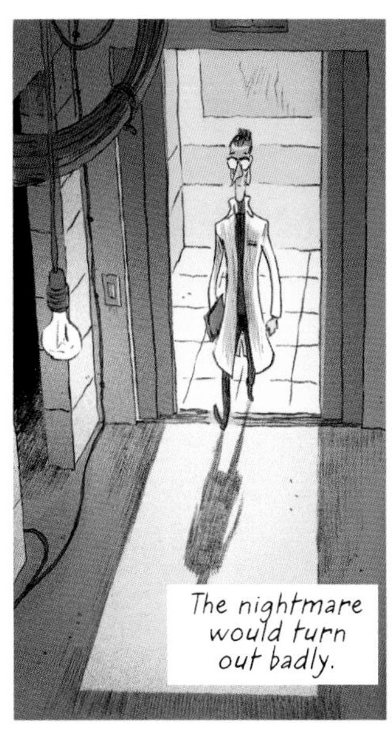
The nightmare would turn out badly.

We, at least, pass through unnoticed.

You can keep me here as long as you like...

...I'll never sleep again for you, Professor!

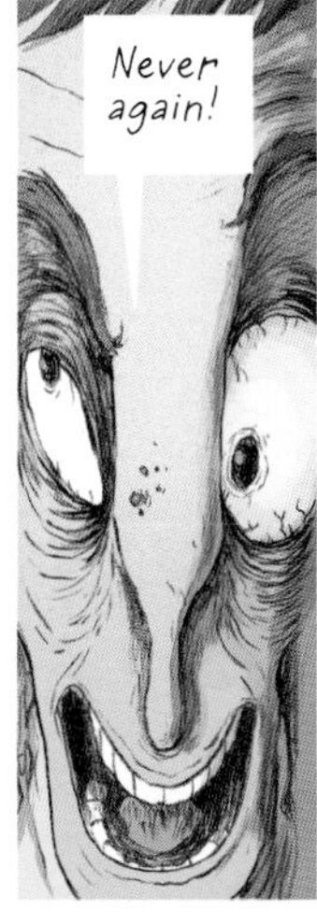
Never again!

Do you hear me?!

NEVER!

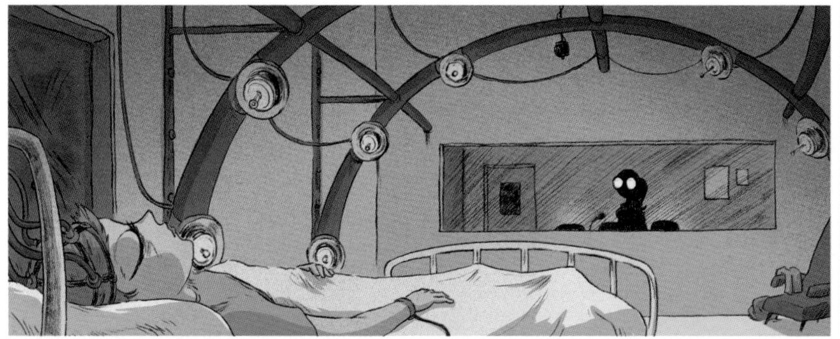

Everything is ready, Professor.

Good.
REALITY 00:00:00
DREAM 00:00:00
Boys, set your Oniricoms.

Tristan, your signals are okay.
Tighten your band slightly, Esteban.

Sarah is going into a deep sleep...

A few more minutes and she'll dream.
Get ready!
DREAM 00:00:00
IMMINENT
Sarah

And don't forget to commit the door's location to memory once you're in the dream...

...to be able to get back out!
We know, Dad!

What does it look like?
Looks like a warehouse.

And it looks quiet.

No monster ready to bust down the door this time.
We have to get it fixed, by the way.

Scheduled for tomorrow.
Go ahead. And good luck...

Okay, we're in Sarah's nightmare.
ZZZ
Walking again feels just as nice each and every time.
There really is something good about being in a dream.
Let's hide the door.
All we need is for one of the characters from the nightmare to end up in our real world.
They've tried that before.
Can you imagine if a dinosaur or an I-don't-know-what made it to the other side?
I'd rather not think about it.
Okay, let's get going!

Our mission is to find Sarah in order to protect her from her own nightmare.
We have to keep her from getting herself killed and especially, to understand the reason for the bad dream.
DO IT YOURSELF
GRILL
RECONNECT
PIERCE
PIERCE
BEAUTIFY
HAMMER
What's she afraid of?
What in her life, her experience, her past, is causing these nightmares?
HEAT
We're here in Sarah's mind, but it's a real world for us.
BURN
HEAT
We can be imprisoned, injured, killed.
And if Sarah awakens suddenly, it'll turn out bad for us...
GRILL
HEAT
Fortunately, though, Professor Angus is keeping watch.
Okay, boys, this is it...
He always warns us, so we make it out in time.
REGISTER

DO IT YOURSELF
CONSOMMER
DRINK
BUY
This snow is weird. It's not cold and... it smells good...
Dreams always warp reality a little...
Eat
This process for entering dreams...
CUT
TRIM
...how did your dad invent it?
SHAV
I don't know eggzhactly.
But before opening the clinic, my dad worked for the government in top shecret projectsh on dreamzh, memory, shleep...

I shuppozhe it'sh connected.
>Gulp!<
What's that wall?
We'll see the big picture from up there.

It looks like there's no way out of the city.
What do the people from here want to protect themselves from?
And where are they?
What do we do now?
Over there! Someone's sending signals.
It looks like Morse Code... it says...
H... E... R... E...
"No—adults—here —no danger"...
Let's go see.
PRAY
REPAIR
Breakfast
Hey! You!

TOSS
GUZZLE
Wait!

Hello? Anyone there?

I'll go see.

I'd love to be able to do that too...

...Crossing through walls...

But okay... You can't have everything!
Dream on!

Don't take a st--
Oh, a kid!
Don't be afraid!
Go inside there. It's for your own good.
I don't recommend you run away!
COME BACK HERE!

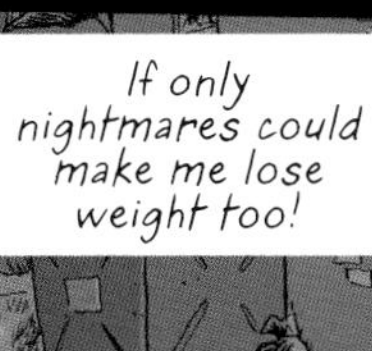

First contact hostile...

The alarm has alerted them.
They're tracking us! They're tracking kids!
What twisted world have we stumbled into? What's going on in your head, Sarah?
Why do adults scare you this much?
She's still in a deep sleep. There's no danger of her awaking.
REALITY 00:02:17
Be very, very careful. If it becomes too dangerous, we'll stop everything!
It's urgent... Police problem...
The police?
Okay...
Elisa!
You know above all else you mustn't disturb me!
Have them wait. I'll be there as soon as possible.

That's where the signals were coming from.

Come in!
And hurry up, for God's sake!

I'm MELANIE.

ARTHUR'S the grouch, and she's Sarah.
We're Tristan and Esteban. We're--
We don't give a crap who you are.

That's her!

The adults spotted you and now they're on the alert.

They're the ones who attracted the adults here! Keeping them with us is dangerous!
They should clear out!
They're staying.

The more of us there are, the more we can protect one another.

We don't know what's going on exactly, it's like we suddenly woke up in this world.
There's hardly any kids left.
There was seven in our group, now there's just three.
The adults are capturing us.
Why?
We don't know.
Nor do we know what's on the other side of the wall or why it surrounds the city.
To protect the inhabitants, no doubt.
Like a fortress.

We have to get out of this city.
There's got to be a door in the wall to get to the other side.
Let's go.

REMEMBER

Got nothing better to do than look at photos?

It's weird. You seem so familiar...
Do I know you?
REMEMBER

I don't know.
I don't have any memories from before these last three years.
Like me!

That's what the sheet in the folder was!
You knew she had amnesia, didn't you?

TING
Esteban, I have to step away... Be careful!
Elisa
COME QUICK!

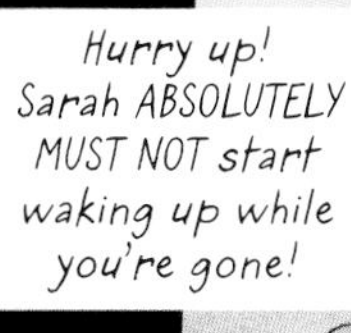
Hurry up! Sarah ABSOLUTELY MUST NOT start waking up while you're gone!

How could men have built such a thing?
It looks like people have tried to climb up it.
If they built it, why isn't there any way up top?
They didn't build it!
MERCY!
WE DON'T WANT TO DIE...
LET US OUT!
PLEASE HELP US
AIDEZ-NOUS
They were kept from getting out.
They're prisoners.
There's got to be some way to get ourselves out of this jail...
Come on, let's go!
KLAK

HELP!
A trap!

HELP ME!

Come on, Arthur!
KRRRR

THEY'RE COMING!
I'm so sorry, Arthur...

DON'T ABANDON ME!

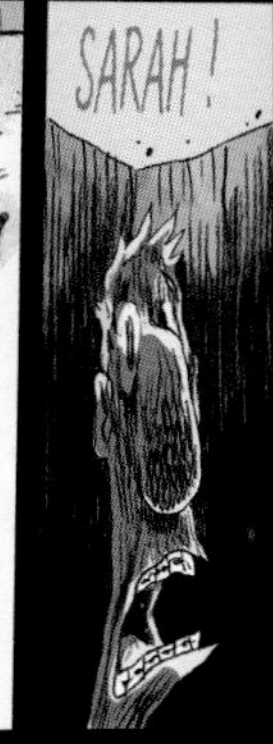
SARAH!

I'm really sorry...
SARAH! NOOO!

Professor Angus?
Police.
ROOMS 101 TO 104
RECEPTION
ROOMS 201 TO 212

We've come for Sarah. Her mother put her in your clinic without the father's consent.

Listen, she's sleeping now and--

And maybe you're thinking we're gonna wait till she wakes up?

We've got other stuff to do!

Wait!
You can't come in here!
STAFF ONLY

That's her.

What's this room?

No! You can't wake her up!
Let us do our job.

Kid? Kid, wake up!

PLEASE, LISTEN TO ME!

WHAT'S THAT?!?
Oh, no...
BLONK
WATCH OUT!
LOOKS LIKE SARAH IS WAKING UP!
CRAP!
THIS WAY!
BRRROOOMMM

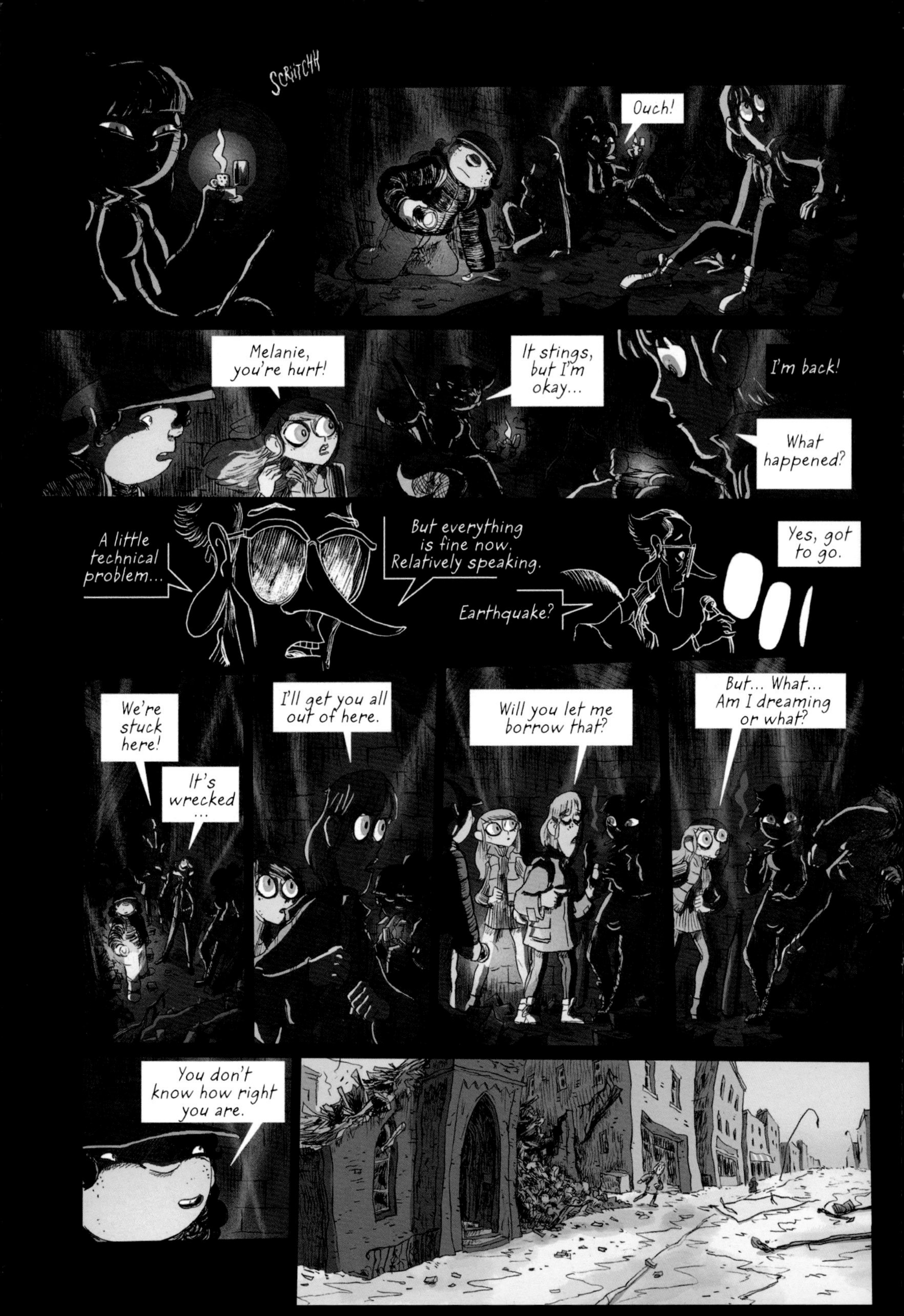
SCRITCHH
Ouch!
Melanie, you're hurt!
It stings, but I'm okay...
I'm back!
What happened?
A little technical problem...
But everything is fine now. Relatively speaking.
Earthquake?
Yes, got to go.
We're stuck here!
It's wrecked...
I'll get you all out of here.
Will you let me borrow that?
But... What... Am I dreaming or what?
You don't know how right you are.

DO IT YOURSELF
BURN
HEAT
PICK
HELP!
HELP!
HELP!
LET US OUT!
ESTEBAN!
Please...

HELP US!
NO!
MERCY!
COMPTEUR
AAAAH!
AAAAH!
AAAAH!
What happened?
Something...
Something came down from the sky and took the kids away.

You saved me earlier.
Thanks.
Sure thing
KLANK
TAKE COVER!
pfff
It's gonna blow!
Pfffffff
Breakfast
SCRITCH
GUZZLE
pfft
WOOOsssSSSHHHHH
BOOOM
PAR
BUY
Hands up!

Why are you hunting us?
What did we do?
You're the ones THEY want. We have no choice...
And as long as you're free...
...THEY will attack us.
Who?
Who's attacking you?
I don't know. But THEY do exist...
THEY really do!
Let us go...
...please.
I had two kids. THEY took them away from me...
Run!
Run away fast before the others get here!
I won't say I saw you.

GATHER
GATHER
An orphanage?
It's so obvious nobody will think of coming to look for us here.
I don't know about you, but I'm hungry.
You coming, Tristan?
TREAT
I think you're kind of cute, you know?
And... if I were handicapped, the wheelchair kind, would you look at me the same?
Of course!
A handicap doesn't change who you are deep down.
Bingo!

...then the sun came back.

The cage was empty and, the kids had floated away...
That's horrible! What was it? Space aliens?
clic

Do space aliens scare you?
SCROUTCH

No, I don't think so.
So, it's probably not space aliens.

Then what is it?
That's what we have to figure out... But in any case, that thing took away all the city's kids...

Sarah has amnesia, she's like me: she doesn't know who her real parents are.
TREAT

That must cause her anxiety. I'm sure it's contributing to her nightmares.
The world of adults scares her, too. They're the ones hunting the kids.
TREAT
And look where we are:

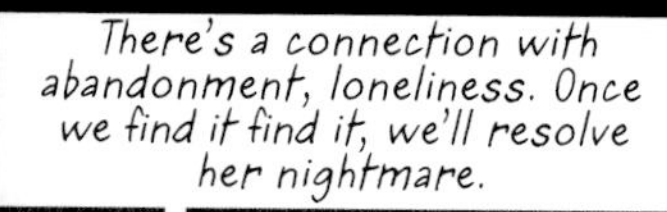
There's a connection with abandonment, loneliness. Once we find it find it, we'll resolve her nightmare.
I'll go see what's on the other side of the wall.
Watch over them.

DREAM
07:58:78
IN PROGRESS
REALITY
00:19:57
Twenty minutes of REM sleep, her dream is in danger of ending soon...
If you don't find the cause of the nightmare very quickly...
...I know.
It'll start again in the following days, and Sarah will keep going downhill.
COME OUT, KIDS!
Sarah
Once her brain activity slows, you'll have only one minute to get out!
One minute for you, but 24 for us!
WE WON'T HURT YOU!
That's always been enough.
Until now...

It looks like there are other cities imprisoned on top of these gigantic structures.
It's so high I can't see the bottom of the abyss.
It's like...

...flowers! You're in a flower pistil!
That's it! Tiny cities inside flowers!
It's not snow! It's pollen!
A butterfly?
That's what blotted out the sun earlier!

And the black tube that carries away the kids is its snout!

You're in an infinitely tiny world.
But why would Sarah be afraid of--
WE'VE GOT YOU!
DON'T COME ANY CLOSER!
Or what?
TRISTAN!
What's happening?
GATHER
The adults have Tristan!
And Sarah's brainwaves are starting to weaken!
The nightmare's going to end!
You must save Tristan AND GET OUT FAST!
I know where they're taking them!

The butterfly...
It's coming...
I...
I must... think.
REMEMB
Why... a butterfly?
The caterpillar, the chrysalis, the butterfly!
It symbolizes time going by, transformation. The passage from one stage to another.
Baby, teenager, adult!
I think I've got it!
Now we just have to wait till THEY come looking for you!
You're the last ones. THEY won't bother us anymore!
OH, YEAH!
THEY'RE GOING TO GOBBLE YOU UP!

ESTEBAN!
Look at me, Sarah!
I know what's scaring you.
You're afraid of growing up... You see your body changing, becoming more and more... adult.
And that world, the world of adults, terrifies you.
Leaving your home one day, being abandoned again, and being on your own...
But you're not alone, Sarah...
He's planting the seed to the solution in the lowest depths of Sarah's mind.
Her brain is reacting immediately!
You're not alone!

It's incredible!
What happened, Tristan?

Who are you two?
Rescuers?
Well, yeah, kinda!
Tristan, we really have to get going.
It's a matter of minutes...
We'll see each other again.
I promise...

Yippee..
Back in the chair...

I was so scared.

Good job!

I'd like to see her again.

You can't meet the patients.
You know full well that's impossible.
It might endanger our secret.

But she's not a patient like the others, is she, Professor?

Who is she? Who am I?
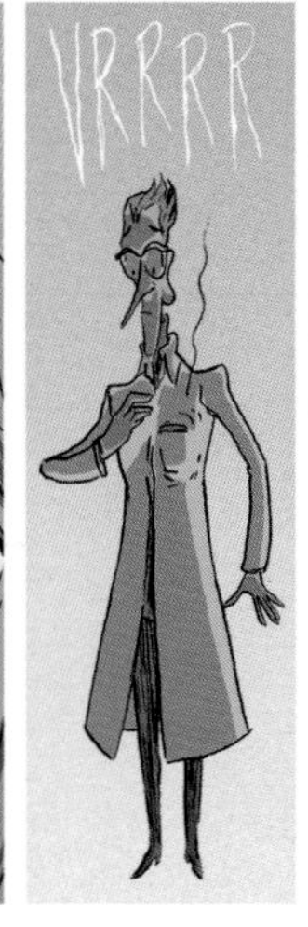
VRRRR

Elisa is expecting me. I have to go...

SLAM

How is she?
PRIVATE
Well.

She remembers her nightmare perfectly. She's no longer afraid.

Now we still have one little matter to resolve...

I'd forgotten about those two.
The police snooping in our business is the last thing we need...
STAFF ONLY

You can't do this. It's not allowed.
I need to see her again, do you understand?

Come in.
NOK
NOK
NOK

Hi...

I'm Professor Angus's son.
I...
DZZZ

This is crazy. You were in my dream but you were walking!

I assure you I'm very real.

As for my legs... They'll never work again.

I'm sorry.
In my nightmare, we were friends.

We can be friends here, too.
I'm new to this city. I'm going to register at the high school.

Maybe I'll see you around?
Definitely. I go to the high school too.
You'll spot me fast. I'm the only guy in a wheelchair!

See you soon, then.

POLICE

Another successful mission!
Another patient saved from the monsters living in their head.

Is something wrong?

It's time I show the two of you.

You've never allowed us in here before.

Are you going to give us a tour of the control room?
No.
Blip

Something else.
Blip
Blip
Blip

Franck Thilliez - Yomgui Dumont - DRAC / August 2017

CONFIDENTIAL
CONFIDENTIAL
CONFIDENTIAL
NOTES
Professeur Angus
TOP SECRET

OBSERVATION

A nightmare often translates an anxiety, fear, or trauma, it stages stories that, sometimes, are violent, morbid, or stressful. No mission into patients' minds will be simple. It will be necessary to keep close watch at every second...

The sleep cycle can be compared to catching a train. If you miss it, you must wait till the next one.

1 TRAIN = 1 SLEEP CYCLE

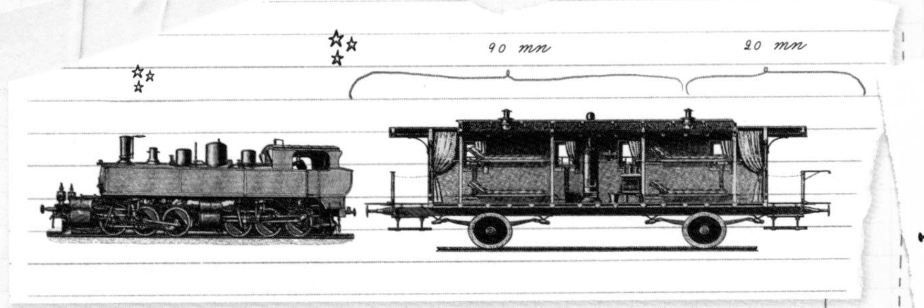

During REM sleep, mental activity is very intense. Certain zones of the brain are subject to a strange activity of rhythmic waves.

That's what I must concentrate on...

REM SLEEP

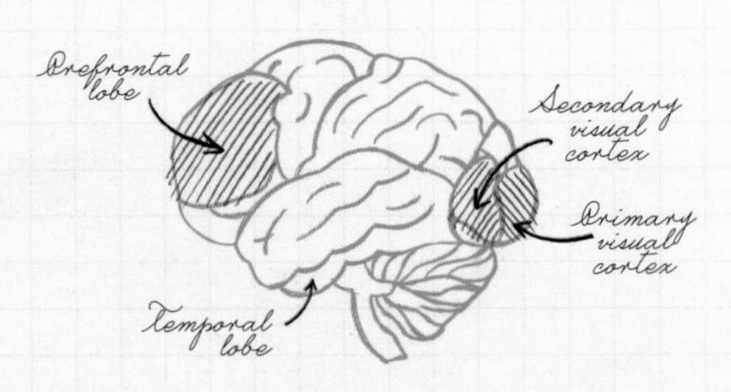

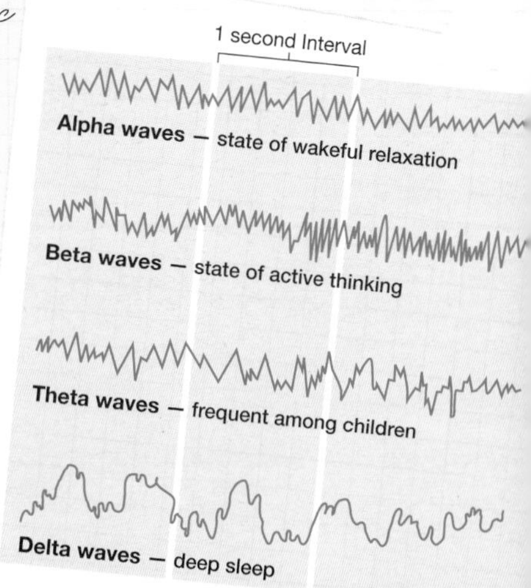

Future travelers absolutely must provide themselves with a backpack containing gear that is vital for accomplishing the mission smoothly.

CHECKLIST

1- Backpack

2- First-aid kit

3- Walkie-talkie

4- Oniricom

5- Water and food

SURVIVAL KIT

1. Healthwise, they'll need a first-aid kit, with bandages, antiseptics, a poison-extractor, acetaminophen, burn ointment, eye drops, a thermometer, little scissors, and suture thread...

2. Cellphones won't work. Walkie-talkies will be perfect if travelers happen to get separated.

3. Water and light, high-energy food, because it's possible travelers won't find anything to eat in certain dreams. They must be able to hold up for about 24hrs.

4. A device that will allow me to communicate with them. I'll call it an Oniricom.

CONTROL ROOM

Access to the control room must be secured. It will be located in the clinic's basement

The Oniricoms must be capable of managing the time differences and the flux of images and voices for our communication to seem smooth.

I'll need at leasst 4 Monitors:

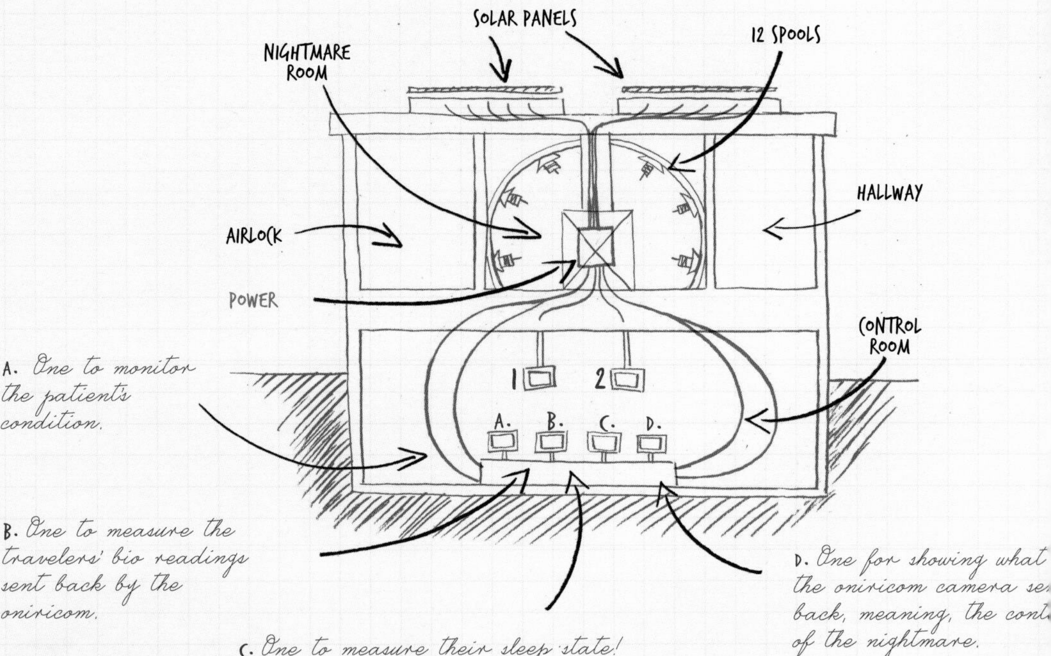

A. *One to monitor the patient's condition.*

B. *One to measure the travelers' bio readings sent back by the oniricom.*

C. *One to measure their sleep state! The sensors connected to the cranium will supply me with a detailed monitoring and will indicate to me the passage into REM sleep.*

D. *One for showing what the oniricom camera se back, meaning, the cont of the nightmare.*

I'll absolutely need two chronometer screens showing time measurement. One of the two will be the time in the nightmare, which, according to my calculations, will pass 24 times faster than here.

LAST NAME: **FRESNEL**
FIRST NAME: **Elisa**
GENDER: Female
BIRTHDATE: 04/10/1984
CIVIL STATUS: Single, no children

RÉSUMÉ

Education
Bachelor of Science, Pre-medicine, 2006
M.D., 2010
Specialist in Neurology, 2013

CERTIFICATIONS
Electroencephalography
Electroneuromyography,
Neurosonology,
Sleep Medicine

Work Experience
~~Pharmacology Institute, University of Nice~~
Sleep Study Center of Greater Lille

Hobbies
Movies, tennis, and reading

Special Skills
Passionate about research concerning sleep, ready to devote all my time to new projects.

No family attachments, I'm very mobile.

I attach high importance to the confidential nature of data.

PERFECT FOR THIS JOB!

I'm so happy we managed to get past our problems, PATRICK...

GO!

For us and for our daughter...

YOU GO, SARAH!

You know, CATHY, she's doing fine now.
It's time for us to forge ahead.

I love you and Sarah so much.

00:07
HOME
VISITOR
56
4
58

I love you too.

LOOK OUT!

00:00
HOME
VISITOR

Nice, Sarah!
That was incred--

You were awesome in the last game of the year, babe!

I don't know what she sees in that ALEX.

I hate this wheelchair!
If only I could stay in dreams!
Don't say that, TRISTAN.

You know full well you can't mistake dreams for reality.

CATHY
& PATRICK
MONIER

What'll happen to her now that her parents are dead?

She doesn't know where she's from, she knows nothing about her past...
Like me.

I have you, and Tristan is like my brother.
But she no longer has a family.

You have to help her, Dad.
I can't. I--

Help her like you helped ESTEBAN!

A few weeks later...
6x2 = 3x...
JULES

... -1 = 62

Grab your pens!
SARAH

Hey, guys!

Where's my room?
Sarah?!

How did you manage it?

Let's just say I pulled a few strings.
I still have connections.

This new processor is even more powerful!

It'll let me create new programs for CASSANDRA...
NO ENTRY
We have to talk to Sarah.

Surely you're not planning on revealing the existence of the Brigade to her?
Of course I am.

I'm even planning to add her to the team starting today...

It took time, but I succeeded in bringing her back, ELISA.
She has her place here. I'm sure she has strong potential.

The more of them that go into his mind, the more chance you'll have of rescuing your wife, is that it?
I miss ALICE so much...

I liked Alice a lot, too.
But that poor LEONARD! You know how I feel concerning him...

He stole her from me. He must return her to me...

But... What... Leonard!

What's happening?
HE'S CONVULSING!

Do you need help?
He just needs air.

It was probably a violent panic attack...
He's calmed down.

I'll send a nurse. GABRIELLE knows how to deal with him.

He's been locked in there for such a long time...

Not for much longer, gentle Elisa.

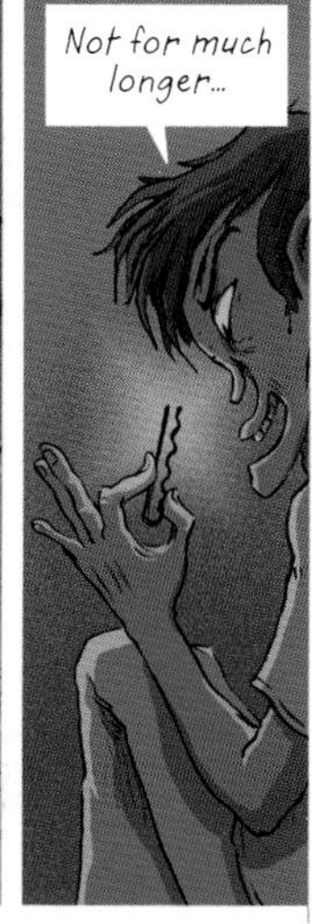
Not for much longer...

Coming, Alice?

We're going to take a little walk.

We call this room the airlock.
You slept in the room just beside it, behind that door.

I can't believe it...
1) TIME PASSES 24X FASTER IN THE NIGHTMARE.
1 HOUR IN REALITY = -> 24 HOURS IN THE
2) NEVER FORGET TO CLOSE DOOR BEHIND YOU!
3) EVERYTHING BECOMES TR REAL FOR YOU ONCE YOU ON THE OTHER SIDE.

When you were in my nightmare, you were real!
You came in from here?
Look through here.

You were in the position of that mannequin that we call Cassandra. Her head is filled with circuits...

...that contain training dreams.
Here, put this on, Sarah.

It's an Oniricohm.
You must never part with it and be discreet when you use it.

Thanks to it, Dad can communicate with us and guide us.
TRAINING
STAGE 1
LOADING

Everything's ready, kids. Cassandra's just waiting for you!
One last thing. We all have a power in the dream.

Tristan regains the ability to walk. I canpass through matter.
You'll have to find yours.

Why the keys?
For security.
Nothing must emerge from the world of dreams!

And that door is your only way to return to reality.

Without it, you would be stuck in the nightmare.
Forever...

Snow!
Last winter my parents and I went skiing...
I often dream of them.
That's because they're still alive in your mind.
If I went into my own dream, could I hug them?
This is crazy!
Nothing must come out of here, not even a photo! My dad told you that!
You didn't take one, did you?
No, no!
What would happen if parts of a nightmare got out into real life?
They'd exist even if they can't exist. That would disturb the balance of our reality.
Distinguishing true from false would become impossible!
EXIT
Concentrate instead! Danger is all around!

That bear could've killed you!
It's lucky we're in a fake dream that freezes as a last resort.
Okay, are you two done? Can we go?
STAGE 2
And what would happen if the sleeping person woke up before we crossed through the door?
We'd be condemned to wander in the nightmare until someone came to free us.
That's good! She's making quick progress!
She's obviously talented... Take a look at this.
Our next patient, NICOLAS GUIRAUD, 14, on the verge of a breakdown.
TRAINING STAGE 3 READY
Anxiety and extreme fatigue due to the same nightmare.
TEST 00H46M39S IN PROGRESS
A night bus, statues, Russian writing...
Gosh, what's going on?
A bad connection, probably. I'll go check...

The Professor will repeat it to you, but you must never talk about this, of course...
Especially not to your boyfriend Alex...
Oh!
Is this new in the program, ALBERT?
No, something strange is happening! COME OUT!
TRISTAN!
AAAAAAAAAHHHH
Sarah...
SARAAAAAAAH!
My god...

It's... impossible!
She can't be dead... Not Sarah...
WE GOT TO GO FIND HER!
It's too late, Tristan!
Cassandra is going haywire. We've got to go!
Sooo, leaving without me?
I think I've discovered my power.
Sarah!
Flying like in my wildest dreams!
Pretty cool, huh?
Return IMMEDIATELY to the airlock, children!
There's something off with the system!
Elisa
Professor! Cables have been deliberately...
... torn out!
What?

I'm coming!

Leonard?

ALICE!
NOOOO!

Okay... Keep searching and keep me updated.

Well? Where's Leonard?
KLING

He stole things in the staff locker room and can't be found.
PATIENT FILES
He's hiding somewhere in the clinic, that's certain... We'll get our hands on him eventually.

Let's go back to the house..
Albert Angus

I'll make pizza for you. You all truly deserve it!

There's something I've got to tell you, Sarah.
Tristan was still little when the accident happened...
What accident?

"From what I know about it, his mother Alice was entering dreams, at the very beginning of the experiment.

"Then, one day, she became trapped in a nightmare.
"Leonard's nightmare.

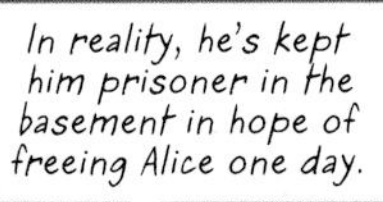

It seems his nightmare is the most terrible one there can be. Once you're inside, you no longer can tell what's real or what isn't. That makes you go crazy,

The Professor doesn't want to risk losing us. Too.

CLEAN!

Can you explain this, babe?

Hey! How dare you go through my stuff!
Give me that!

Sure looks like "wimp on wheels" isn't as handicapped as he's pretending to be.

Is he doing that so people will feel sorry for him?
Get out of here!

Go on, stand up!
Show how you're able to stand on your legs and fight!

LEAVE HIM ALONE, MORON!

I HATE YOU! I DON'T WANT TO SEE YOU ANYMORE, ALEX!

Why did you do that? You're an idiot!
Stupid dork!
He's lying! Don't you all get it?

He's faking it! I saw him standing!
What happened?
Nothing, I slipped...

Any word on Leonard?
Traces of him in the kitchen...
Otherwise, nothing. Nobody's seen him.

But we have work this evening...
A new patient.

They'll pay for that!

Everything's ready on my end.
Nicolas is about to dream.

I locked the door to avoid any bad surprises...
Good...
Get ready, kids!

My goodness, Tristan...

You weren't snacking before the mission, by any chance?
It wasn't me this time.

The coast is clear.

Go ahead...

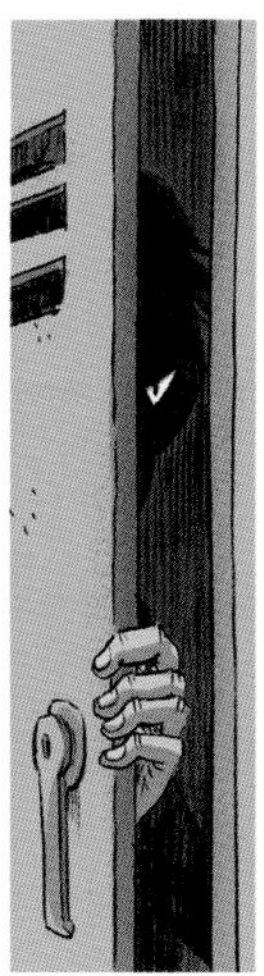

Leonard?

IT'S HIM!
Out of the way, blondie!

STOP HIM FROM ENTERING NICOLAS'S NIGHTMARE!

He...

He's gone!

Forget the mission!
You must get Leonard out of there at all costs before the end of the nightmare!
If he's trapped inside...

...Mom will be even farther from us...

...Trapped inside Leonard's mind...

...with himself trapped inside Nicolas's mind.

How are we going to find him again?
It looks so big. He can be anywhere!
Don't worry, Sarah... all nightmares have limits...
Leonard can't be hiding very far from here.
Look at the date: we're in 1986...
сегодня вечером большой фейерверк
26 апреля 1986 г
According to Nicolas's file, it's Russian.
It says: "Tonight, big fireworks."
In any case, it looks nothing like a nightmare...
Did you see that old-fashioned fairy?
It's the 20th century...
It's sure to be old-fashioned!
What if I flew up to take a look?
Good idea, but it's too risky to go flying off here.
It's not our dream, so we must be careful, remember!

Privet.*
What's your worst nightmare?
I'm in a world where everything is made of candy and sweets.
But I don't have a mouth...
I'm arriving in front of a house belonging to my real parents.
I know they're waiting for me behind the door.
But the closer I get, the farther away the house is. I can never reach it.
What the--

What madness is this? Transformed into statues?
It's suddenly gotten dark.
Here, too.
And look around us. These shabby walls... It's like everything got old instantly.
Petrified.
Good God!
Sorry, ma'am.
It's like ash...
Time seems to have stopped in April 1986...
... at 1:23...
Come look, guys.
26/04 1986
01 23
All those shapes... frozen.

abandoned.
The plants have taken over again...
by in a fraction of a second.
our present.
Be quick, children... Please... Bring Leonard back to me...
These people tried to run from something.
And they were all petrified.
Like in Pompeii.
How come we didn't get changed into ash statues?
We're intruders in Nicolas's mind. His subconscious hasn't noticed us yet, but that won't last long.
Look out!
Quick! Take cover!

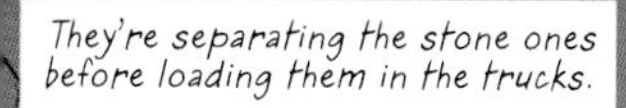

*Russian for "This one!"
**Russian for "But we're a long way from the beach!"

Okay, this is nice and all, but I'd like a carousel ride.
You think there's any chance of that, bud?
You're not very talkative...
Later, dude!
They're gone... Let's go.
Now what?
TOUR
Weird, I feel like I've seen this before.
Me too...
I know this place.
Look! It's Nicolas, our dreamer!
He looks completely lost.

mix in with them!
No reception in this at all here.
Hey! Don't leave!
Pretty light!

It's not picking up.
Do you think the bus will come back for us?
This city is fascinating, isn't it?
Were you on the bus, too?
Yes.
Do you know what we're doing here?

No idea...
I woke up just before we arrived without knowing where we came from.
What are they saying about it?
From what I understood, they paid to come here.
They talked about visiting the restricted zone "Pripiette"...
Pripyat?
April 26, 1986! Why of course!
My God, you'r
right beside..

...Chernobyl!
Isn't that the thing that blew up a long time ago?
We studied it in our history class...
The worst nuclear disaster of the last century!
What disaster? What kind of watch is that?
Who are you talking to?
Yikes! Sarah is attracting too much attention to herself.
Nicolas will panic.
Get ready for a paradoxical cataclysm!
Who are you?
WHERE ARE WE?
Am I dreaming or is it raining crabs?

СПОРТ
СПОРТ
Nicola
Calm down...
We're with you...
You must be more unobtrusive, Sarah!
If Nicolas understands there are intruders in his dream, his mind will react violently!
I... I'm sorry.

I've definitely come here before...
Me, too. It's like I'm having flashbacks.
Something awful is going to happen.
Worse than crabs raining down, you mean?
Much worse, yes, I fear...
No, I don't have a Ukrainian background.
I'm just learning Russian in school.
And do you know this city?
Pripyat? Or Chernobyl?
I've seen some reports before on the nuclear disaster, that's all.
What's with all these questions?
Stop grilling him!
I thought I was very clear!
Nicolas isn't the priority anymore!

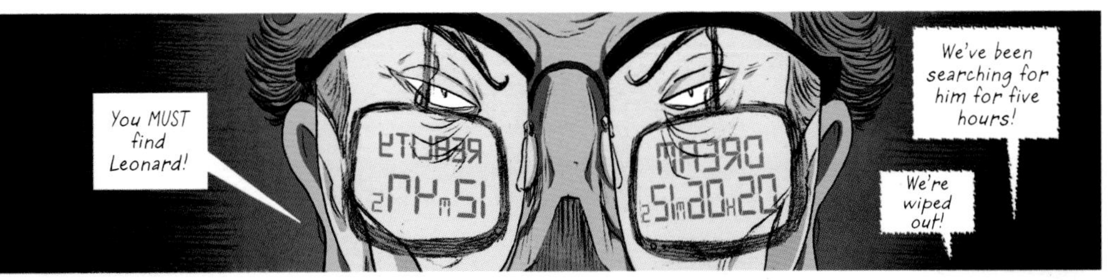
You MUST find Leonard!
We've been searching for him for five hours!
We're wiped out!

DREAM
REALITY
12m55s
And it's freezing tonight! We have to rest a little...

Esteban is right. They're not machines.
Look at Nicolas's readings. They're stable again. You can let them catch their breath...

Out of the question, Elisa.
We don't have time!

For God's sake, Professor, how far will you take this?
Besides, Sarah's not ready yet. You surely saw that!

You're endangering everyone.

Keep your comments to yourself, Elisa!
Return immediately to Nicolas!

And get ready to prolong his REM sleep to the maximum!

Dad?

Yes, son?
All these people living in Pripyat...
... did they die after the nuclear power plant explosion?
Most of them, yes.
It took months, years, but yes, they died... Even after the evacuation...
They developed illnesses linked to the radiation released by the reactor. Genetic mutations, cancers.
That's horrible!
Mankind often wants to do good, but terrible things sometimes are the result...
And could we get contaminated?
There's more radioactivity in the restricted area, that's for sure.
But you're not staying there long enough, so there's nothing to fear.
FRED! DAMIEN!
WHERE ARE YOU?!
Problem?
Our friends went to find wood for the fire. It's been an hour...
And we heard shouting.
LOOK. THAT LIGHT OVER THERE!

Maybe it's Leonard...
Or mutant wolves! Or radioactive monsters!
Let's go see.
GZTZZ
Guys?
Fred?
Good Lord!
Dami...
LET'S GET OUT OF HERE!
DTZZTZ
What about the others? We can't leave them!
They're just dream characters! We aren't, Sarah!
COME ON!

So that's it...
A bus brings people here, abandons them...
And something transforms them into stone.
But what?
We're all gonna die!
No! We're here to protect you.
To protect me?
Let's just say we're protecting each other...
AAAAHHHH
AAAAAHHHH

In the Ferris wheel! Quick!
No way...
LEONARD!
Who is he? A friend of yours?
Go away!
You're going to blow my hideout!
SHE's going find me!
SHE...! I remember now!
SHE's coming! SHE's going kill us all!
Who are you talking about?
THE FAIRY!

GZZZT
DZZT
DZZT
HELP!
CRRRRRR!
CRRRRT
HELP!
CRRR
CRRR
CRRR
Are you scared of fairies?
If that thing's a fairy, then YES!

She's spotted us!
We're screwed!
You all go hide up there. The building where it all began.
I'll slow her down and meet up with you!
HURRY!
What's going on in your head, Nicolas?
Is radioactivity what's scaring you?
What does it symbolize for you?
Something that can't be controlled?
Sickness?
Contamination?
Death?

What a nightmare!
She's searching for us...

DREAM 09H10M36S

REALITY 22M56S
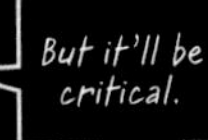

The dream can keep going thanks to Elisa's boosters.
23 minutes...
We've never gone beyond 30 minutes.
But it'll be critical.

So, that's it for Mom?
I'm sorry, Tristan...

I'm so sorry...

I know it's prohibited, but...
What if we brought Leonard's statue back with us into reality?

Yes, yes! We have nothing to lose by trying!

What about the fairy?
We can spot her easily by the traces she puts off...
We can avoid it.

I haven't seen the fairy in over a quarter of an hour.
She must have gone away.

Let's go.

Don't leave here and rest, Nicolas. Nothing will happen to you.
Okay. I'm exhausted anyhow... Good luck.

Albert, who brought Nicolas to the clinic?
His father.

Can you check if his mom is still alive?

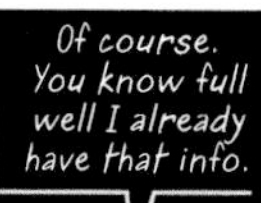
Of course. You know full well I already have that info.

She is.

But we don't care about that!

Get Leonard and come out!

He's even heavier than me!

GZZTT

THERE SHE IS!

Come! We're out of time!
Tristan, it's too late!
Get in! Quick!
Where's Sarah?!
She was right behind me!

SHUT THAT DOOR!
KLONK
KLANK
KLONK
This way, beautiful!
Sarah! What are you doing?
Come bac
right now
We can't abandon them...
Neither Leonard nor your wife!
Dang! The gas mask guys are already there!
ONA IDET! POYDEM V LAGER'!*

Sarah, Sarah, Sarah...

Esteban?!

You've no business here!
And you think going into people's minds is allowed?
Elisa let me in.

Elisa?!

But you know nobody is allowed to enter the basement without my authorization.
Elisa? Do you hear me?

Well? Have you made your decision?
You don't turn down a dream job in brain study at the prestigious McGill University, Miss Fresnel.
Elisa? Who are you talking to?

ELISA!
I'll call you back as soon as possible.

Excuse me, Professor. I accidentally cut the sound.
Where were we?

Looks like the fairy has calmed down.
How long has the dream time been?
About 26 minutes.

The timing's close, Sarah knows that. She'll return fast by flying.
What's the use?
Do you really think she can bring Leonard back all by herself?

This is madness!
The Chernobyl nuclear power plant!
The same buses... What are they doing there?
I can't believe it. I'm in the middle of a closed down nuclear power plant.
Why couldn't it have been an island paradise instead?

PSSHHHH
It's like the stone is melting!
They're not completely fossilized!
It's like their coated in stone.
PSHHH
Where are they taking them?
They're loading them in the buses.
PRIPYAT TOUR

This nightmare is sick stuff!

Okay, I get it... It's always the same people getting petrified in a loop...
They take them to the fairy so she'll transform them into statues...

As if they were feeding her.
The masked men pick them up then reanimate them before dropping them off in the city...
And it starts over and over again...

Okay... Let's think...
The fairy is the radiation that keeps destroying and taking lives, even decades later...

You should call Nicolas's parents.
See if there's some history of contamination or illness in his family.
You're right.

Secrets always resurface in one way or another.

The nightmare will end soon!

Hurry it up, Sarah!

*Russian for "Stop!"

KLONK
KRIK KRAK

I was so scared!

That was a close call!

Nicolas is awake now.

You saved them, Sarah!

You saved both of them...

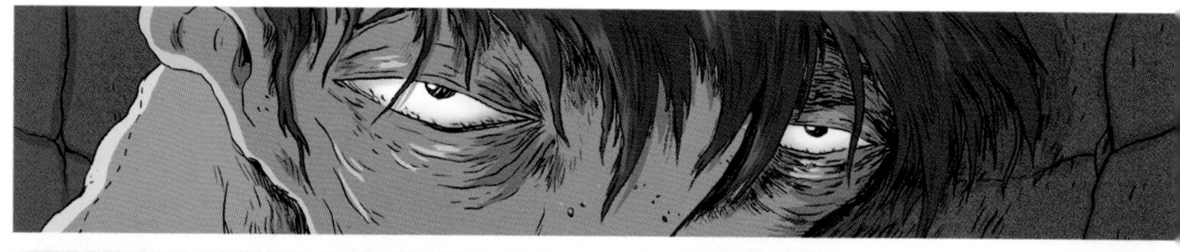

NOOOOOO!

Seeing him like this eats away at me.

But I have no choice, Elisa.

You understand me, I hope?
Whatever you do, it's too late to go backwards.
What's done is done.

Experimenting is failing before making an advance.
Even with the best intentions in the world, nobody is infallible.
Neither you nor this program.

And to answer your question: yes, I understand you.

WE no longer have a choice.

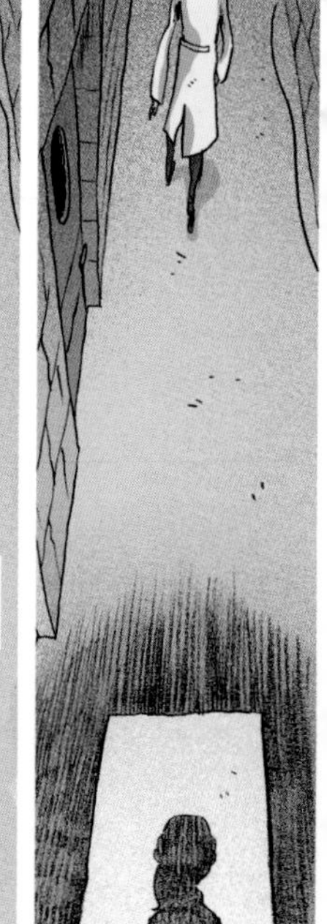

BIP
BIP BIP

RING RING
What did I do with my keys?

Yes, hello?
Hello, Mrs. Giraud?

I just spoke with Nicolas's mother.
Esteban was right.
NO ENTR

When her son was 9 years old, she had cancer that was treated with radiotherapy.
It saved her!

The radiation treatments destroyed the "crab," like they say in France...
But it weakened her, made her lose her hair...

He probably thought it was slowly killing his mother when it was just the opposite.
She admitted to me that the two of them had never talked about it.

A lack of parent-child communication...
Dad and Mom always refused to tell me where I was from...

I'm going to explain everything to him and he'll get better.
Nicolas will recover.

Jeez, Sarah, you really gave us a scare!

All that adrenaline, I LOVED IT!

And flying is awesome!

Almost as good as walking...

Esteban?

You there?

DOSSIERS PATIENTS

Sarah... Sarah... Where are you?

ESTEBAN

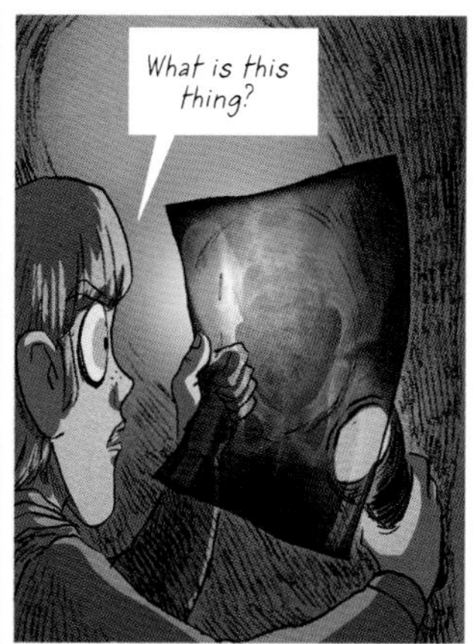
What is this thing?

LARGE ANGIOMA ON STOMACH..
A-65 / PROFILE
NOTHING TO REPORT
OK

SUBJECT A-65
MEDICAL FILE
SLEEP CLINIC
SLEEP CLINIC
LAST NAME
UNKNOWN
FIRST NAME
(SUPPOSED)
ESTEBAN
PARENTS

DATE OF BIRTH
DOESN'T EXIST
BIRTHPLACE
DOESN'T EXIST

PARENTS
FATHER
DOESN'T EXIST

This is impossible!

DRACULA
STEPHEN KING

I...

I'm...
SUBJECT Nº A-65
CONCLUSION
SLEEP CLINIC
ESTEBAN IS A CHARACTER WHO ESCAPED FROM NIGHTMARE #65.
HE DOESN'T EXIST!
SLEEP CLINIC
ALBERT AN
RECOMMANDATIO

I'm a nightmare character.

Franck Thilliez - Yomgui Dumont - DRAC / AUGUST 2018

SUBJECT-65

CONFIDENTIAL

ESTEBAN

MEDICAL FILE
SLEEP CLINIC
SLEEP CLINIC
ALBERT ANGUS
HEIGHT 4'10" / WEIGHT 79 ½ lbs.
A-65 / PROFILE
NKNOWN
POSED)
ESTEBAN
DATE OF
DOESN'T EXIST
BIRTHPLACE
DOESN'T EXIST
MOTHER
DOESN'T EXIST
LARGE ANGIO
ON STOMACH...
OBSERVATIONS
Good health overall. Organs in the expected places.
Measurements of about an eleven-year-old child
at the moment of his discovery. Blond, blue eyes.
Birthmark on his naval, in a crescent shape.
LIKE ALL THE OTHERS!
I.Q. 138
Normally developed brain
Brillant intelligence tests.
Suffers from characteristic acute retrograde amnesia.
1/2
Brain waves
OK
cardiogram
NOTHING TO REPORT

SUBJECT N° A-65
SLEEP CLINIC
SLEEP CLINIC
ALBERT ANGUS
ESTE CHARACTER WHO
ESCAPED FROM NIGHTMARE #65.
HE DOESN'T EXIST !
RECOMMENDATIONS
Esteban must be kept under control and
not stray too far from the clinic.
Adoption required by any means necessary.
CALL JOUBERT
As a precaution, a tracker was placed near his
left kidney. This tracker is functioning.
SIGNATURE :
CONFIDENTIAL
Albert Angus

WATCH OUT FOR PAPERCUTZ 

"To sleep, perchance to dream—ay, there's the rub." – *William Shakespeare*

"Welcome to my nightmare. I think you're gonna like it, I think you're gonna feel like you belong. A nocturnal vacation, unnecessary sedation, you want to feel at home 'cause you belong." – *Alice Cooper*

Welcome to the frightful first volume of THE NIGHTMARE BRIGADE "The Girl from Déjà vu," by Franck Thilliez, Yomgui Dumont, and Drac, brought to you by Papercutz, those sleepless souls dedicated to publishing great graphic novels for all ages. I'm Jim Salicrup, the Editor-in-Chief and somewhat the equivalent of Professor Angus at the Papercutz dream factory. I'd like to talk a little bit about dreams and nightmares, and I hope this won't put you to sleep…

Dreams and nightmares have fascinated us since there's been an us—collective humanity. There really are places that study our sleep and what our brains are doing while we're asleep. And creative types such as William Shakespeare, who was really referring to death in his quotation above, and Alice Cooper have enjoyed exploring the dark side of our dreams. Fictional characters, such as *Freddy Krueger*, have been visiting our nightmares regularly, even if we didn't reside on Elm Street. And comics have been exploring dreams for a long time, from Windsor MacKay's *Little Nemo in Slumberland* to Neil Gaiman's *Sandman*. Considering how often our dreams have been invaded by these characters, it's about time we have THE NIGHTMARE BRIGADE on our side!

Generally, I can't even remember my dreams. I'll wake up, and it's like I hadn't been asleep at all. But there certainly have been exceptions. Recently I spent a week and a half dog-sitting Benji and Athena at my brother's home while he and his family were away on vacation. I made a dumb mistake, I binge-watched a scary TV series called *Evil* while staying in an unfamiliar house. Sure enough, I had a scary nightmare. It didn't bother me too much, (although I did start to feel spooked being in that house alone) as I generally don't find horror shows that scary. Believe it or not, most "horror" movies or TV shows tend to just make me laugh.

There was a dream I had as a young boy that I still remember vividly. As a comics-loving kid growing up in the Bronx in the 60s, it was often tricky finding the latest comicbooks on the newsstands. There were no comicbook stores back then, so it was a challenge trying to maintain a complete collection. One night, I had what I later learned is a lucid dream—a dream that you believe is real. In that dream, I found a drugstore in a nearby neighborhood that carried comics and on the comicbook racks were the new issues of all my favorite comics. When I finally woke up, I was a little confused. I think I thought what happened in the dream must've happened the day before. Boy, was I frustrated when I finally realized that it was all a dream! In my mind, I saw all those new comicbook covers so clearly, that I thought they had to be real. But alas, they were not.

There was another "dream" I had back then as well. This was more the kind of dream about one's personal goals and future. My dream was to work in comics and live in Manhattan. And believe it or not, it came true! I can honestly say, I'm living the dream.

But enough about me! Back to THE NIGHTMARE BRIGADE… if you enjoyed the first two chapters of this exciting new series as much as we did, you're probably already eager to get to the next chapters. Good news—your dream will be coming true soon and you'll return to The Angus Clinic and further explore the mysteries that have been set up in this premiere volume, in the second volume of THE NIGHTMARE BRIGADE, coming soon from Papercutz. So, until then, may I wish you… sweet dreams?

Thanks,
Jim

STAY IN TOUCH!

EMAIL:	salicrup@papercutz.com
WEB:	papercutz.com
TWITTER:	@papercutzgn
INSTAGRAM:	@papercutzgn
FACEBOOK:	PAPERCUTZGRAPHICNOVELS
FANMAIL:	Papercutz, 160 Broadway, Suite 700, East Wing, New York, NY 10038

Go to papercutz.com and sign up for the free Papercutz e-newsletter!